MY PIG AMARILLO

For Sonia

Copyright © 2002 by Satomi Ichikawa
First American Edition published in 2003 by
PHILOMEL BOOKS,
a division of Penguin Putnam Books for Young Readers,
345 Hudson Street, New York, NY 10014.
Philomel Books, Reg. U.S. Pat. & Tm. Off. Published simultaneously in Canada.
First published in France as *Mon Cochon Amarillo* in 2002 by l'école des loisirs, Paris.
Manufactured in China by South China Printing Co. Ltd.

Text set in 15-point Grantofte Regular.
The art was done in watercolor.

Library of Congress Cataloging-in-Publication Data
Ichikawa, Satomi.   My pig Amarillo / Satomi Ichikawa.   p. cm.
Summary: Pablito, a Guatemalan boy whose pet pig Amarillo has disappeared, uses a kite to
send him a message that he still loves him.
[1. Pigs—Fiction. 2. Pets—Fiction. 3. Kites—Fiction. 4. Guatemala—Fiction.] I. Title.
PZ7.I16 My 2003   [E]—dc21   2002007318
ISBN 0-399-23768-2
3 5 7 9 10 8 6 4 2

MY PIG AMARILLO

Satomi Ichikawa

Philomel Books • New York

One summer day, my grandpa arrives home with a tiny pig on a leash.

"Pablito, it's for you," he says.

I am so excited, I do not know what to say.

I decide to call him Amarillo because of his color. *Amarillo* means "yellow" in my language. "Don't be afraid, my little yellow pig," I tell him. "You'll be my best friend."

He climbs on my back, and scratches me!

I make a beautiful hut for
him. He can sleep in it.
Is he tired?
Sleep, then, little pig.

Little by little, Amarillo grows. We play together every day.
Everywhere I go, he follows. We love to splash in the mud
best. He is my best friend, just like I told him.

One day, I come home from school and, just like I do every day, I call, "Amarillo!" But he doesn't come. His hut is empty. I call him again, and again, even louder, but he still doesn't come. Where could he be?

"Mama! Anna!" I shout to my mother and sister, who are weaving cloth. "I can't find Amarillo anywhere! Have you seen him?"

"No, sorry, Pablito," they say.

I run to my father, who is driving a
bus. "Papa, have you seen Amarillo?"
"No, Pablito," he answers.

Oh, where is he? What's happened to my pig? I cannot eat.

"Where are you, Amarillo? Where did you go? And why did you leave?"

I cry into my pillow. "I am waiting for you to come back, but you don't."

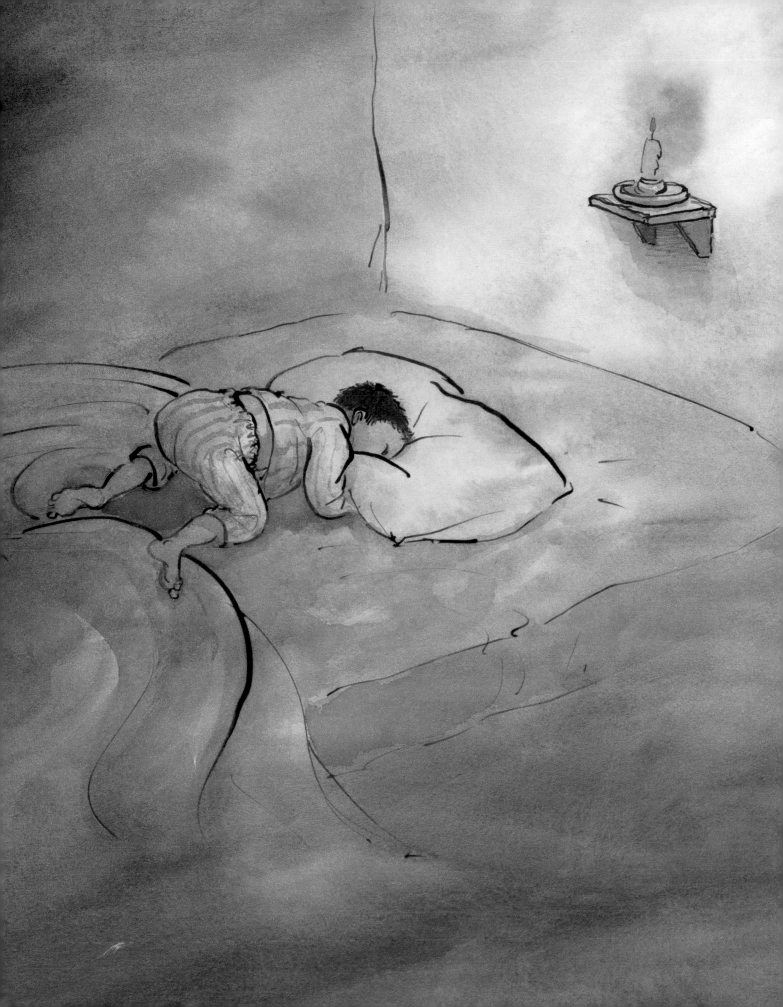

The days pass and still no
Amarillo. One morning, my
grandpa hands me a wooden pig,
which he has carved himself.
    "It's for you, Pablito," he says.
    It is a yellow pig with spots,
just like Amarillo. He is very
kind, my grandpa, but I want
my real Amarillo.

Grandpa says if we can't find Amarillo, he could have had an accident and may have died. These things happen, Grandpa says. But if this is the case, he is in peace with angels in the sky. He must be happy up there.

But me, here, without him, I am so sad. My heart feels like it will break open.

"Here, when people are sad and they miss those who have died, do you remember what we do?" Grandpa asks me. "We send them a message in the sky so that we can communicate with them."

"A message?" I ask.

"We fly kites on All Saints' Day. That's how we send them messages," Grandpa explains. "Do you want to try to do that, too?"

Yes, I want to try. All Saints' Day is coming
soon. I have to prepare my kite.

My kite must fly as high as possible so that
Amarillo gets my message and knows I am looking
for him.

Maybe he will send me a sign.

Finally, All Saints' Day is here. Everyone arrives in the cemetery.

Fly, fly, my kite! Fly toward Amarillo!

My kite soars over the fields and keeps going up, over the mountains. Then it disappears into the clouds.

"Oh, look, Pablito! Up there, above the mountain, see that enormous cloud?" cries Grandpa, pointing.

"I see it," I shout. It is my pig, Amarillo. "He's smiling right at us!"

Suddenly, I don't feel sad. I have found my Amarillo!
I wave my arms and cry as loud as I can, "I see you,
Amarillo! There you are! I love you and I'll love you forever!"